For Luke O'Brien, whose first tattoo was Ferdinand the Bull. –A.M.

For Nici Ploeger-Lyons, my tattoo buddy. –E.W.

With thanks to Bill Snell for the inspiration.

Text copyright © 2016 by Alison McGhee.
Illustrations copyright © 2016 by Eliza Wheeler.

Library of Congress Cataloging-in-Publication Data:

McGhee, Alison, 1960- author.
Tell me a tattoo story / by Alison McGhee ; illustrated by Eliza Wheeler.
pages cm
Summary: A father tells his young son the story behind each of his tattoos.
ISBN 978-1-4521-1937-3 (alk. paper)
1. Fathers and sons—Juvenile fiction. 2. Tattooing—Juvenile fiction.
[1. Fathers and sons—Fiction. 2. Tattooing—Fiction.] I. Wheeler, Eliza, illustrator. II. Title.
PZ7.M4784675Te 2016
[E]—dc23
2015002694

Manufactured in China.

Design by Kristine Brogno.
Typeset in Bodoni Egyptian.
The illustrations in this book were rendered in
India ink with dip pens and watercolors.

10 9 8 7 6 5 4 3 2 1

Chronicle Books LLC
680 Second Street, San Francisco, California 94107

Chronicle Books—we see things differently.
Become part of our community at www.chroniclekids.com.

TELL ME A Tattooe Story

BY ALISON MCGHEE

ILLUSTRATED BY ELIZA WHEELER

chronicle books · san francisco

You wanna see my tattoos?

Why, little man, you always
want to see my tattoos.
Here we go then.

This one, well, this one's from
my favorite book that my mom
used to read to me.

Did she read it to me over
and over and over?

She sure did.

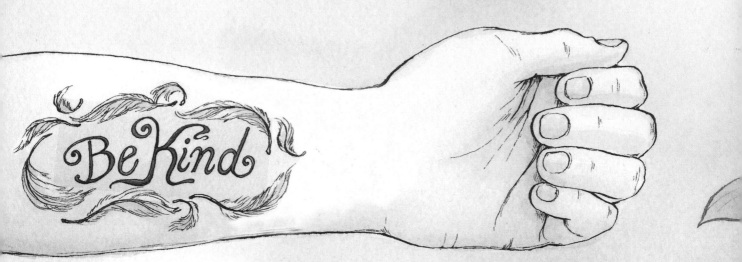

This one?

This one says "Be kind."
That's something my
dad used to tell me.
And I want to make sure
I always remember it.

This one?

This one reminds me of
the day I met a pretty girl.

What made her so pretty?

That's a good question, little man.
I'd have to say it was her smile.

Have you ever met her?

You sure have.

This one, well, this one's from
the longest trip I ever took.

Did I miss home while I was there?

I sure did.

This last one?

Just a little heart, is all.
Those numbers inside it?

Just somebody's birthday,
I guess.

Whose birthday?

Oh, some little man I know, is all.

What do you mean, this one's your favorite?
This dinky little heart?

I wonder about your taste in tattoos, little man.
I really do.

But I'll tell you a secret if you come real close.

That one's my favorite, too.